For my sons, Kwesi and Kip, with
many thanks for all they have
taught me

CHAPTER ONE

In the week before Daniel and his girlfriend's wedding his life changed forever. The problem wasn't marriage because he and Louise had lived together for three years since leaving college. Getting married would not change much.

The big change was instead due to something which Daniel simply could not have foreseen: a sudden shock. Before this he thought of himself as just a normal person, living a normal life. And if anyone had asked him what *normal* meant the answer would have been simple. To Daniel 'normal' was his own way of life.

On the other hand, this was only half the answer. From his first day in school Daniel had known that he was different which was why, his mother had said, the bullies picked on him. Daniel agreed. There was only one

1

way to keep out of trouble, he thought, and that was to pretend to be just like the rest of them. Normal.

He was twenty-six, the same age as his girlfriend, Louise, and taught at a comprehensive school in North London. Louise was also a teacher, and they lived together in a ground-floor flat. At the weekends, they normally went out to the cinema, or for dinner with friends. During the summer they sometimes drove down to Devon to stay with her parents.

By this time doing the same things as most of his friends seemed like second nature to Daniel. Sometimes he did feel that he was living under a sort of disguise but also he couldn't really work out how to change things. He couldn't even guess what he wanted them to change to. On the surface, his life was happy but deep inside he still felt angry and confused. He shared most of his thoughts with Louise, but this problem he found impossible to explain to her. Going out with Daniel was the only thing that had marked her out from her family and friends. Apart from that, Daniel realised that they lived in much the same way as her sister and cousins. She called it a normal life, where living with Daniel was a stage, after which getting married was the right thing to do. And Daniel agreed it was what a normal couple would do.

But there were still some people who regarded Daniel and Louise as an odd couple. Louise looked a lot like Daniel's mother in that she was tall, blonde and pretty, with pink skin which flushed easily. Daniel, meanwhile, was just the opposite, with a light brown skin and curly black hair.

He often wondered about his father. Perhaps he looked like him, but there was no way of telling as Daniel had never even seen a photograph of him. He only knew that his father had come from

Nigeria, and had died before he was born.

After they decided to marry, he tried to tell Louise about how this made him feel. 'I wish my father was here,' he said.

'Why? Do you miss him?'

'No. I never knew him, so I can't miss him.' He was struggling to find the right words. 'But there is something missing.'

He knew a lot about what he was missing. Part of it was a feeling of safety. In primary school, he had stood his own ground against the bullies in the playground. Mostly, not having two parents did not matter. It was different, though, when other kids' dads turned up to watch them playing sports or to take them home. When that happened, he sometimes had felt a rush of longing so strong that he could hardly control the tears springing behind his eyes. And when other kids teased him the way they were always doing to each other, he had the same crazy thought: You wouldn't do that if my dad was here.

As he got older, he stopped thinking like that. Instead his absent father gave him a new problem. Many of the people he met seemed to think that the colour of his skin gave him some kind of special access to what they called 'black culture'. Mostly it didn't matter. He got tired of explaining that he had been born and brought up nearby, and that he knew nothing about African drums or voodoo or the blues. It got really boring when he had to say that to kids he had known for most of his life, but most of his friends weren't that stupid. It was the teachers who kept on about 'his culture' who annoyed him.

The teacher who got on his nerves most was said to be an expert on black culture. When he talked to the black kids he always seemed to be talking about the Carnival and rap music. Daniel was known as a quiet boy who studied hard, and he became one of the teacher's targets. After a while, though, Daniel began to get the idea that the man seemed to know about his absent father, and saw him as some kind of social problem. Sometimes he came home seething with rage after one of the teacher's talks. 'He thinks,' he told his mother, 'that if you're black you have to be some kind of rebel. And as far as he's concerned, being a rebel means wearing a hood and rapping. And if you're really cool you can go to jail or walk the street, without a job.'

At school Daniel hid his anger. He knew by now what kind of future he wanted. He knew also it would count against him if he was seen to reject the man's attempts to teach him about 'your own culture'. The issue came to a head at the start of the sixth form. Daniel chose to study a book of classic English poetry, instead of the black poet who had visited the school. On the day Daniel made his choice the teacher gave him a sad look, as if he had been badly let down.

Sometimes Daniel thought that this was one of the reasons he had chosen to become a teacher. At least, that is what he told Louise when she asked him about it.

'I want those kids to be able to do anything they want to do. They don't have to be what other people expect them to be.'

That was what he felt when he started. Three years later he wasn't so sure about anything. On the day his life changed his father was the last thing on his mind. Later on, though, it struck him that this meeting had always been waiting to happen.

It was a routine part of Year 10 work on a local history project.

The project involved visiting the libraries or the local museum, and looking up the history of old buildings. Daniel's pupils enjoyed this, partly because it got them out of the classroom.

On the first day of the project someone suggested talking to old people who had lived in the district for a long time. Daniel said it was a good idea and he would think about it. What he didn't tell them was that, a couple of years before, a few of his pupils had turned up without notice at a nearby home for the elderly. The result had been mayhem. One of the staff, taking them for muggers, had called the police. Daniel spent most of the day getting the group out of the police station. Then he'd had to explain to their parents; and after that he'd had to placate an irate head teacher.

'Never again,' he'd said, but now he found himself thinking that was unfair.

During the break that day he discussed the problem with Judy, the head of his year.

'The thing is to choose a few people.' She paused. 'With care. Talk to them first, then you let the little horrors loose on them.' She laughed and made a funny face. 'The last thing you want,' she said, 'is not being able to get to the altar because you're getting the kids out of jail again!"

She winked. Daniel sighed. He had been teased without mercy for the last couple of weeks. The closer the date of his wedding came, the worse it got. It was the reaction of his women colleagues which surprised him. He had known nearly all of them for a couple of years. Most of them had never been more than friendly, but almost as soon as he announced that he was to get married, a few had begun to flirt with him. The fact that he didn't know quite how to respond made them even more wicked. Something about weddings, Daniel thought, made people excited.

Judy hadn't reacted in the same way as most of the others. Instead she had made a dry comment about how young he was. She was only about thirty, not much older than Daniel. On the other hand, she had been married and divorced. No one knew the details, but it gave her the status of a cynic, who could speak her mind without offence. She was friendly enough to Daniel, but sometimes he wasn't sure how much she liked him.

'Why don't you get them to talk to old Brownjohn?' Judy suggested.

'Who?'

'John Brownjohn. He was deputy head and he's lived around here for years. He won't mind.'

That was true enough. Daniel telephoned and was invited to drop in after school. As Judy had predicted, Brownjohn seemed more than pleased to help.

He was about sixty, thin and fit. His head of grey hair was going bald, and he had a deep, friendly voice. Daniel guessed in the first minute that the pupils would like him. Even better, he seemed to know every fact there was to know about the district.

Daniel relaxed, preparing himself to sit and listen politely to Brownjohn's memories. The last thing he expected to hear was a memory which would change everything he knew about himself.

CHAPTER TWO

Brownjohn had seemed a little wary of him at first. His manner changed when he was clear about what Daniel wanted. In the next couple of hours, Daniel heard everything he might ever have wanted to know about the district.

It was a fine, bright, summer's evening. They sat facing the French windows which were open to the garden. The fading sunshine slanted in, glinting off the top of Brownjohn's bald head. In the distance, over the tops of the apple trees, Alexandra Palace shimmered against the sky.

'Lovely, isn't it?' Brownjohn said, as if he'd been reading Daniel's mind. He got up and strode to the window, his cup of tea still in hand. 'Two hundred years ago, this was all farmland and countryside. Now look at it. But the gardens are still lovely.'

Daniel nodded, trying to look as if all this was still holding his interest. In fact he was thinking it was time to go and was working out his exit line. At the same time he was wondering how he would describe Brownjohn to Louise. Suddenly he was tired, and it was harder and harder to focus. Brownjohn, meanwhile, was still talking about the history of the district. 'All this used to be empty fields,' he said. 'The bits in between London and the next town. We're close to the highway. The old turnpike was over there. Get them to think about the names of the places. They're full of history.'

Daniel nodded again. He already knew the local history, but it seemed rude to say so. Instead he shifted about in his chair, trying to signal that he was about to leave. Brownjohn took no notice and instead seemed to be talking faster, skipping quickly from one subject to another. 'They named these streets after famous admirals,' he said. 'Cochrane, Collingwood, Nelson. I used to live there, in Nelson Avenue.'

Daniel sat up, some instinct telling him that the words were important. 'Nelson Avenue?'

'Yes. Number 12.'

'Not Number 12?'

Surprised, Brownjohn turned to look at him. 'Yes . . . Number 12. I lived in the top flat and rented the ground floor to some students.'

Daniel took a moment to think about it. The entries on his birth certificate flashed through his mind. 'I was born there,' he said slowly.

Brownjohn laughed, amazed, and not yet certain Daniel was serious.

'It's true,' Daniel said. 'That's where I was born.'

'How old are you?' Brownjohn asked.

'Twenty-six.'

Brownjohn stared at him, taking in what Daniel had said. 'I know you,' he said slowly. 'Your parents lived there. I can see them now.' He paused as if finding the right words. 'A mixed couple.'

'You're sure?' Daniel asked.

'Quite sure. Wait a moment.'

He went out of the door and Daniel waited, his mind in a turmoil. If the old man was right, he would have known his father. There would be a lot he could tell him that he had always wanted to know.

Suddenly Brownjohn was back,

carrying a photo album with a faded red cover. It was already open and he held it up in front of Daniel and pointed to an old photo of a couple, standing in a garden. The man was holding a baby.

'That's you,' Brownjohn said.

Daniel gazed at the photo, bending over to get as close as he could. The woman was Sarah, his mother, younger than he could remember, but certainly his mother. The man was tall, the same height as Daniel. There was a strange pattern in the fading colours. It was as if the skin tones, black, pink and brown, had been carefully matched.

Daniel's heart seemed to skip a beat. Before this he had never seen a photo of his father. Once, in the middle of an argument with his mother, he had let loose his anger about that.

'How could you not have a photo of him?' he had shouted.

'My life was different then,' she

replied. 'I travelled light. Things got stolen. Once I lost all my belongings. All that got lost.'

'I can't understand you, Mum,' he had told her, his rage turning to sadness.

'I liked your father,' Brownjohn said. 'He used to joke about my name: John Brownjohn.'

He laughed. Daniel didn't think it was that funny but he smiled to be polite.

'How is he?' Brownjohn asked, still chuckling at the memory.

Daniel looked at him, puzzled. 'Didn't you know? He died before I was born.'

Now it was Brownjohn's turn to look puzzled. He stared at Daniel. 'But I saw him a couple of years ago. He came up behind me in the High Street. "John Brownjohn," he said. "John Brownjohn!" and he laughed. I'd know that laugh anywhere.'

He stared at Daniel, taking in the young man's look of shock. 'I'm sorry,' he said. 'I don't know what's going on, but if that's your father, he's still alive.'

CHAPTER THREE

Daniel fired questions at Brownjohn for another hour, but the old teacher hadn't much more to say. He kept repeating that Daniel's father was alive, then he corrected himself. 'At least he was alive a couple of years ago.'

The first name was Chris, he told Daniel, but he couldn't call to mind the surname.

Daniel frowned, thinking about it. Chris was not the name his mother had given him, but he guessed the old man was somehow confused.

By now he could see that Brownjohn was tired and bored. Daniel said he was leaving, then asked to borrow the photo.

Brownjohn handed it over with a speed which hinted he was glad to get rid of his guest. Daniel didn't notice.

As he left, his mind was already busy with the questions he planned to ask his mother. He went straight to her house, which was a semi-detached in the north of the borough.

Daniel had lived there for most of his life. Sarah had married while he was still in primary school. Looking back on those days, Daniel recalled that moving and leaving the home he'd always known had been one of his fears after his mum told him about getting married. Another fear had been that she would leave him, to go off with the man she was about to marry. This was one he had never told her about. As it happened, they didn't move. Instead his new stepfather came to live in the house with them. Daniel's room became his refuge, somewhere he could safely ignore the couple.

He had never told his mother how angry he had been in those days.

It was already past ten o'clock by the time he got there. As he walked up the garden path he hoped his stepfather would be out. More than he ever had in his life, he wanted to see and talk to his mother alone. He wanted to show her the photo, then look into her eyes and ask her for the whole story.

Thinking back on it, he realized how little she had told him in the past. When he was younger he used to press her for stories about his dad. What he wanted was the sort of stories other kids told: something funny or even weird he could talk about on the way home from school. 'That's just what my dad's like,' he imagined himself saying.

However much he asked, though, she was always vague. What she told him made him more curious without giving him anything he could get his teeth into. They had met when she had just started work as a teacher.

'What happened? Daniel would ask. 'Where was he?'

Someone had introduced them. She couldn't remember who it had been. They hadn't known each other long before she found she was pregnant. It had been a matter of weeks. All Daniel's questions about the details met with the same answer. She didn't know. His father had no family. He had been brought up in care, the same as herself and her sister Nancy. There was no one to worry about; they had been enough for each other. When she told him she was about to have a baby, he was happy.

He had been a photographer starting on his career, working for newspapers and magazines. The week she told him about Daniel he was offered a freelance job. They thought it was a good omen. They didn't think about danger. They were young and death seemed far away. He was only going to be away for a month. She thought that all the questions could be answered when he got back. But he never did come back. A week later she was phoned to say that he had been shot and killed. There was no more.

Daniel opened the door with his key and went in quietly. As he had hoped, George his stepfather was slumped dozing in front of the TV. His mother was sitting in the little room behind. Through the half-open door he could see her peering at the computer screen, fingers busy on the keys.

Seeing her like this, it struck him that she was still pretty. She was almost fifty, but her figure was still straight and slim. The photo he had borrowed from Brownjohn was twenty-five-years-old. It seemed such a long time, and he wondered, for a moment, how living through all that time had changed his mum. In the picture her blonde hair had been longer, swinging down to her shoulders.

Now it was cut short, and if you looked closely you could see the streaks of grey. Those were only outward changes, he thought.

'Mum,' he said quietly.

She looked round, and smiled when she saw him. 'Hello, love. I was just thinking about you.'

Normally, when he visited like this, they would chat about what he was doing but this time he couldn't wait. He took the photo out of his pocket and held it up in front of her.

'Who is this, Mum? Tell me who this is.'

She took the photo from time, her smile fading. She held it up to the light, turning away from him, studying it with care. 'Where did you get this?'

She had her back to him and he couldn't see the look on her face.

'It doesn't matter,' he answered.

'Just tell me who these people are.'

I don't know,' she said slowly. 'Who is it supposed to be?'

He paused for a moment, amazed at her reply. 'That's you,' he said harshly. 'Don't you know your own face? And that man is "Chris". And that baby is me.'

She held the photo up to the light again. Watching her closely, he thought he saw her hand tremble, but it was gone in a flash.

'I really don't know,' she said. 'It *looks* like me. But I don't remember it at all. And this man . . . I never knew a Chris who looked like this. I've never seen this man in my life.'

CHAPTER FOUR

'But that's you, Mum,' Daniel persisted.

For a moment he felt unsure about where he was, like someone lost in an alien landscape.

'Yes, I suppose it is me,' she said. 'Yes. It's me, but I don't remember.'

She turned around and looked at him, smiling. 'Well, I did look like this once. A long time ago.' She paused, thinking about it. 'It looks like the garden at Number 12. You were only a few months old.'

'Is that my dad?'

She raised her eyebrows in surprise. 'No. I don't know who that is.' She looked again. 'There were always people coming and going,' she said. 'I guess he was a friend of someone's. Maybe Nancy.'

This was her sister Nancy. The two of them had been orphans, brought up in a series of foster homes. His mum didn't like talking about those days. She had once told him that she felt guilty about the fact that he had no grandparents. She knew nothing about his father's parents, which meant that they were all alone in the world.

'Never mind, Mum,' he had said. 'I'm used to it.'

'So was I. Until you came along. It was always just me and Nancy.'

Nancy had been the pretty one, she always said, who had married well and died young.

Now when she mentioned Nancy he looked at her sharply. 'I thought Nancy had married and gone off before I was born,' he said.

His mother sighed and looked away again. 'She was on holiday. She came and stayed with me for a bit in Number 12.'

This was another thing she didn't like talking about. Nancy had married into a posh family. Her husband became a diplomat and they travelled a lot. When she died in a car accident his mother had taken him to the funeral. He was only little, but he sensed her dislike of the people there. Later on he realized that he had been the only black person present. He thought also that his mother's rage had been something to do with the way the posh mourners had behaved towards them. She told him later that when she went to sit in the pew reserved for the family an usher had stopped her. Instead of letting her sit where she wanted he had showed her to a seat at the back. After all that, someone in the churchyard had said something to upset her. She wouldn't say what it was, and he could only guess.

'They were just a bunch of snobs,' was all she would say.

Nancy's husband married again, not long after. Then he had gone into politics. When his mother saw his picture in the newspaper she would throw it aside, as if seeing him still made her angry.

'Where did you get this photo?' she asked him again.

'A man I went to see today. I didn't know before, but he used to live at Number 12 when you lived there.'

'At Number 12? What was his name?'

'John Brownjohn. He was a teacher.'

'Oh. I remember him. John Brownjohn.' She laughed. 'He's still around?'

'He is, yeah.'

Quickly, he told her about his visit to Brownjohn and what the man had said about his father.

She held up the photo and glanced at it quickly. 'And you thought this was your dad?'

'That's what he said.'

'Silly old prat,' she burst out. 'He didn't really know us. He was all right, but we kept ourselves to ourselves. We didn't want him going around talking about us.'

Daniel nodded. That was how he and Louise were with the couple who lived in the flat above him.

'Come here,' his mum said.

She got up and hugged him, stroking his hair the way she used to do when he was little.

'Never mind,' she said. 'That man could never stop talking bollocks.'

He laughed. Then something else came to mind. There were some other things he wanted to ask her. He cleared his throat and sat down.

'About my dad,' he said. 'Can you remember if he had any special problems with his health? Like sickle cell. Things like that.'

She stared at him, her forehead creasing up in a frown. 'Why do you ask?'

For a moment he didn't answer. He and Louise had decided not to tell anyone before the wedding. Now he didn't know what to say. His mother saved him the trouble.

'She's pregnant, isn't she?'

'Yes.'

For some reason—he didn't know why—he had been worried about how his mum would receive the news.

'Don't worry,' Louise had said.

'When your mum gets used to it, she'll be thrilled. Trust me. Most women love babies.'

Daniel had believed her, but in the moment that he told his mother he was certain that her reaction was nothing to do with being thrilled. Instead, as he told Louise later, he could have sworn that the look which crossed her face was pure, naked fright. In a second she had caught herself and begun to smile, but for an instant he had seen nothing there except fear.

CHAPTER FIVE

He told his mother quickly about Louise finding out she was pregnant. She watched him, smiling, as if she knew what he was going to tell her. He smiled back, telling himself that he had been mistaken about her first response. Of course Louise had been right, he told himself. After all, they liked each other, and a baby would be the family that both he and his mother had missed.

'It happened,' he told her, 'and, once we knew, we thought everyone would be pleased if we got married.'

'That was something that always worried me about you,' she said. 'You so much love to please.'

He frowned. She always said this, and it always got on his nerves.

'Don't get me wrong,' she said. 'I like Louise, but I wish it hadn't turned out like this.'

'I thought you liked her,' Daniel said. Suddenly he was angry.

His mother's look was intense, as if she was trying to work out what to tell him. 'I wasn't certain,' she said, 'if you liked her because she liked you. I can see she loves you, but you're different.'

Suddenly what his mum had said when he told her he was moving in with Louise came back to him. 'What about her family?' she'd wanted to know.

He had told her there was no problem, but he had never been sure. Louise's mum and dad had been friendly enough. Her father had been some kind of manager, and now they lived by the sea. That was all. He had kept their visits short and resisted getting any closer to them, telling himself that he couldn't be sure how long he would be with Louise. The ties between them were about their life in London. Somehow the life she'd had before seemed like a threat but she had seemed hurt when he tried to explain this to her.

'I don't *want* to know them,' he told her. 'I don't want to be part of their nice, quiet life.'

At the back of his mind had been the fear that this was the life she wanted. Although he had tried to hide his feelings of doubt from his mother, somehow, though, she guessed. In any case, he'd known

31

already that she would dislike Louise's parents. She hadn't yet met them, but he knew her well enough to guess. In her mind these were the same boring, narrow-minded people from whom she'd had to protect him. 'Straights', she called them.

'You do go for these nice, sensible young ladies,' she used to say, teasing him.

The strange thing had been that in his own mind he'd agreed with what she felt. On the other hand, something about the fact that she didn't approve had pleased him.

'I know what I'm doing,' he had told her. 'You're just a sucker for romance.'

Now he could see that she was somehow troubled.

'Don't feel you have to get married,' she said, 'just because of the baby. This is your life, and her life. A long time. You should decide what you want to do, then think about the baby.'

'We're getting married,' he told her. 'And that's the end of it.'

His mother watched him, frowning a little.

Knowing that she had already guessed that he had doubts made him more angry. 'You've got these ideas about romance,' he told her. 'It's like you want me to go out and fall madly in love with some crazy girl. Well, I'm not like that. I want a mortgage and a home and I want my kid to grow up feeling safe. I don't want him to worry his whole life about what's going to happen next.'

She winced. He had told her this before when he was angry, and she knew he was talking about his own childhood. These outbursts hurt her more because usually he was so controlled. When he was like this she knew that he meant every word.

'If that's what you want to do,' she said. 'Let's not argue. I just want to be sure you'll be happy.'

'I know what I'm doing,' Daniel

said.

It was only later on that Daniel would admit to himself that this was very far from the truth.

His mother smiled broadly as if to make up for her first response. Then she clapped her hands, jumped up out of her seat and hugged him again. 'I'm so glad for you,' she said. 'I told George this was coming.' She held his hand and pulled him into the front room. 'George,' she called out. 'George. We've got some news.'

It was another half an hour before Daniel could escape. He had the odd feeling, though, that his mother had been hiding something. Part of how she had reacted, he thought, had been sheer relief at having a good excuse to avoid talking about his father.

'I believe her,' he told Louise when he got home, 'but there's still something funny about it. The way she looked at the photo.'

He had been sure that there was

something his mother had not told him, but he couldn't guess what it might be. It was just that he knew her so well. When he was little and they only had each other, she had called him 'her little friend'. Sometimes, at bedtime, when she read to him, he would sense that she was tired or sad. At such times he would hug her tight, as if he would never let go.

'My little friend,' she used to say. 'What would I do without you?'

That was why he could sense how upset she was when he showed her the photo.

'It's just strange that she doesn't remember,' he told Louise.

Louise had been watching a video, already dressed in the T-shirt and baggy pyjama bottoms she wore in bed. Now she sat curled up on the sofa in their living room, her eyes intent on Daniel as he paced around, talking.

That's how she was, Daniel

thought. When it was needed he could count on her to listen quietly, taking it all in before she said anything. It was a habit which reminded him of his mother. That was not the only thing. They were both teachers, and to most people their slim figures and blonde hair made them look alike. At first sight, strangers were likely to assume the two women were related.

Daniel didn't mind. He agreed there was a likeness, but to him it wasn't about their looks. It was more to do with the way they both acted towards him. Apart from that, they weren't at all alike.

'If she's not telling you all she knows,' Louise said gently, 'maybe she has a very good reason.'

He made a frustrated gesture. 'I can't think what the reason could be.'

'I can think of lots of things,' Louise said. 'If he beat her up, for example, she might not want you to know.'

Daniel frowned, and, before he could stop himself, gave her an angry look. Somehow it had begun to annoy him that Louise was taking his mother's side.

'I'm not saying that's how it was,' Louise said quickly. 'But you have to agree that it might be something like that.'

Daniel looked away, gazing into space and thinking about it. He hated the idea that his father might have been harsh and cruel, but he knew that it could have been that way.

'I guess you could be right. But, even if he did, she didn't have the right not to tell me about him. She had no right.' He was shouting, and he took a deep breath, trying to calm down. What he'd told his mother flashed through his mind and he turned to Louise, knowing that he would have to tell her sooner or later. 'I told her about the baby.'

'Oh. You promised. I haven't told my own mum yet.'

'I'm sorry,' Daniel said. 'She guessed.'

He should have known that she would guess when he started asking about illnesses his father might have passed on. He braced himself, but if the thought crossed Louise's mind she kept it to herself.

'Well, it doesn't matter. They'll all know soon enough. Only tell her not to let on she knew before anyone else.'

They went to bed well after midnight, having spent over an hour talking about his mother. Daniel still couldn't guess what was going on, but he had made up his mind about one thing. He didn't tell Louise, because he knew she would argue, but he now knew what he had to do.

In the morning he would begin tracking down his father's footsteps, and he would not rest until he knew the truth.

CHAPTER SIX

Daniel didn't change his mind the next day, but the sign he was looking for didn't turn up until that weekend.

Sarah telephoned on the Friday night to say that she and George would be away for a couple of days. 'That will give you a chance,' she said, 'to clear out some of that stuff in the shed. If you make enough space in there I can get rid of some of the junk in your old room.'

'It's not junk, Mum.'

'Yes it is. Anyway I can do with moving things around. I want to fix that room up in case you and Louise come to stay.'

'Why would we do that, Mum? We only live fifteen minutes away.'

There was a pause. 'All right. Just in case.'

On Saturday morning Daniel let himself into his mother's house bright and early. At first he took care to sort through the boxes and bags in the shed. For years he had been putting things he didn't need there. Now looking through them was like digging into the story of his life.

In one corner, there were boxes of toys, picture books, comics and games. In another corner were bags full of old clothes. These held his old football kits, pair after pair of running shorts and shoes, old school blazers, and heaps of sweaters and trousers he had grown out of long ago. Beside them were an old games console, a battered computer he had swapped for a chess set he'd bought at a car boot sale, and his old mountain bike with his twelve-year-old football boots hanging on the bar. Then there were piles of paper, old school essays, sheets covered by his writing in black ink, photocopies and posters. On top of all these were bulky textbooks, stacks of printed notes from his college days, and old

CDs.

Daniel went through all of them.

After a couple of hours he was tired, hot and sweaty, but he didn't stop. It was as if he wanted to make sure there was a balance between his hard work and the thing he meant to do later. By halfway through the afternoon he had a big pile of black plastic bags stacked outside the shed.

He stopped, went into the house, washed, and changed into an old shirt from his room. Then he went into the little room where he had talked with his mother during the week. This was where she prepared her lessons and worked on the computer.

He was looking for the small filing cabinet in which she kept her private papers. He found it where it had always been, in the corner of the room near her desk. It was locked, also, as it always had been.

Sarah kept the key on her key chain, but this was no problem for

Daniel. When he was fourteen she had bought him another cabinet just like it for his private things. He had lost the key within a few months, but he had soon found out how to open the lock without it.

Now he took out a long thin screwdriver he had found in the toolbox in the shed. One twist of the lock and the cabinet was open. Inside there was a stack of folders, and he took them out, one by one, keeping them in order. There was nothing in them except notes, household bills, a few letters, mostly from George. He took care not to read them. The last one was the thinnest, and this was the one he opened first. It held a few newspaper cuttings, the paper going yellow and faded. All of them were about a car accident. There was a blurred photo of a young woman, and the name under it was Nancy Benson, his aunt.

He was putting the cuttings back when he saw the photo. He took it out of the folder and turned it round, but somehow he already knew what he would see.

It was a couple with a baby—a black man and a young white woman. The woman was his mother. This time she was the one holding the baby. The other adult in the picture, his arm around her shoulders, was the man Brownjohn had called Chris.

CHAPTER SEVEN

Seeing the photo was perhaps the biggest shock of Daniel's life. He packed the folders back in, moving quickly. He knew that his mum and George were far away, but he couldn't help feeling that they could come back at any moment and catch him. He left the house in a hurry. Somehow, knowing that his mother had lied, he couldn't bear to stay there.

At the flat, Louise had just come in from the shops. She was busy putting things away in a cupboard, but something about the way Daniel carried himself made her pause and stand up to look at him. 'What's wrong?' she asked.

'The photo,' he blurted out at once. 'She's got the same photo. It's nearly the same anyway. It must have been taken at the same time.'

'Hold on,' she said. 'How do you know this?'

Quickly, he told her about searching his mum's files and finding the photo.

'You shouldn't have done that,' she said.

'If I hadn't, I wouldn't know, would I? She's got it well hidden, and she lied to me.'

'If it's the same photo, she could have forgotten about it.'

'You're joking, aren't you?'

'All right,' Louise told him. 'No

point in arguing about it now. But what I said before is still true. She must have a very good reason for hiding it.' She paused, thinking about it. 'What are you going to do? Will you ask her why?'

Daniel shook his head. 'How can I? I'm not going to believe anything she tells me, for a start.'

'You have to do something,' Louise said. 'I know you. You won't just forget about it.'

'I've been thinking about it. First, I don't want to tell her that I searched through her private things. That isn't going to help. Second, if she straight out lied to me, you're right that she's got some reason and she is not just going to tell me. I've been thinking my whole life that my dad was dead. If I had known, I would have found him, one way or another. Maybe he doesn't even know I exist.'

'He was holding you in the photo,' Louise pointed out quietly.

Frowning, Daniel walked over to

the window and looked out at their patch of garden. It was a sunny day and the rose bush at the back was blooming for the first time, but somehow his mind couldn't take in what he was seeing. 'All we have is Brownjohn's word. And what does he know?' he asked, without turning to look at Louise. 'But even if he does know about me and he doesn't even care, I still need to see him.'

'You're talking as if you believe he's alive and he's out there somewhere.'

'I don't know,' he said. 'That's the whole point. But I have to find out.'

He had a plan of action worked out. It was clear that he couldn't rely on his mother to tell him about the photo and the man with her. He would have to find out for himself. 'I'm going to phone old Brownjohn,' he told Louise. 'I'm not sure I got all he knows out of him.'

Brownjohn's voice on the telephone sounded cautious and

46

withdrawn, as if he wasn't sure that he wanted to talk to Daniel.

'It's about my dad,' Daniel said point blank.

There was a silence on the other end.

'I don't know any more than I've told you,' Brownjohn said after what seemed a long while. 'They were a nice couple. I didn't know their friends. I met the sister once or twice, but that was all.'

'That was useless,' Daniel said to Louise when he hung up the phone.

'Maybe you should just wait and talk it over with your mother.'

Daniel shook his head firmly. Louise didn't get it, he thought. All this wasn't simply about finding his father. The way his mum had acted meant that she had some kind of trouble which she had kept to herself during the whole of his life. She needed help, and going over to accuse her of lying wouldn't help. The only way to fix things was to find out what was going on.

'I'm going back to the house,' he told Louise.

CHAPTER EIGHT

Daniel went straight to his mother's little study. Then he began sorting through the stacks of files and papers. He was looking for something which had a link with the past.

On the way there he had been working out what he knew about his mother's life. All of a sudden, it seemed strange that, before this, he had asked very few questions. Of course, he had always wanted to know more about his father, but his mother had always been there. In his mind she had always been the same.

When she got married he had been jealous and angry, but after a while he had learnt to get along with the man, and they began getting to know each other. George's first wife had died some years before, and he had no children. He was good-tempered and friendly towards Daniel, took him to the park so he could ride his skateboard, went with him to the movies and the video rental at weekends. Daniel never saw him angry. That was the sort of person he was. All he wanted, he told Daniel once, smiling, was a quiet life.

Daniel took the hint. The trouble was that he could never forget that George had come between him and his mother. The other problem was that George was a white man, fair haired like his mother. Daniel could never pretend that he was his real father, or even forget that he was not. He could never confide in George, either, about some of the feelings he had as he grew up. In spite of all this, though, he began to treat the man as a friend. George, in his turn, kept out of any quarrels between mother and son. The problem was that the way they were was a kind of surface.

When Daniel thought about it he always remembered one occasion when he had almost screamed at George. This was when he had been told that George was going to marry Sarah. They had taken him for a lunch at a nearby restaurant. This was an unusual event, so he knew something was coming, and he had time to prepare himself. On the way home, they were walking past the tube station and saw a scuffle. There were two black youths standing against the wall of the station being searched by two policemen. There were another six policemen standing around. A couple of police cars were drawn up behind them. Suddenly one of the youths threw himself sideways and tried to run. In an instant four or five policemen had thrown him to the ground and were on top of him. They pinned his arms behind him. The other boy was screaming with all the strength of his lungs. There was a group of young black men standing around and they were shouting too. It was like a wall of sound, the background to the deadly struggle in the middle of the crowd. The last thing Daniel saw as they walked by was the police forcing the two boys flat against the wall.

The scene made Daniel upset and angry. He had no idea what the boys had done or why they were being arrested. It was the sight of the crowd of white policemen, the look of rage and despair on the boys' faces, the way they struggled, and the shouts of the crowd. For a moment he wanted nothing more than to see the boys escape. It didn't matter who they were or what they had done. In normal times Daniel would have talked about the scene with his mother. In front of George, though, there was nothing he wanted to say.

Inside the house he stood in the

kitchen with his mother as she put the kettle on.

'Did you know those boys?' she asked him.

'How would I know them?' he said sharply.

'I thought maybe school. I would guess they come from around here.' She paused. 'I shouldn't say it but I'm glad you don't know them. I don't know what I'd do if I saw something like that happen to you.'

She looked as if she was about to cry.

'Don't worry, Mum,' he said. 'I keep out of trouble.'

Before she could answer George came through the door.

'It was a very unpleasant scene, that,' he said. 'But I'm sure they must have done something.'

'You don't have to do something,' Daniel told him. His tone was sarcastic and George raised his eyebrows. 'They stop you, and if you don't keep your temper anything can happen.'

George was about to answer and Daniel saw the warning look that his mum shot across the room.

'Maybe,' George said.

Right away Daniel knew that George didn't believe him. He also knew that George would never grasp how he felt about what he had seen. From that time Daniel knew how things would be.

It was a bit like the way that he felt about Louise's parents. When he met them he had to put on a kind of polite act, which meant that everyone could keep their real feelings to themselves. Daniel had lived like this for most of his life. Almost all of the white people he knew had an idea of one kind or the other about who he was. By the time he was a teenager he was already fed up with having to explain that he was someone different. He was fed up, also, with having to explain that who he was meant that he saw the same things from a different angle. With Louise and most of the girls he went out with, sex had been a sort of bridge between knowing and not knowing. With other people, like his fellow teachers and his stepfather, he had learnt to keep a distance.

Standing in the empty house Daniel wondered whether George knew about the puzzle he was trying to solve. For a moment he thought about asking, then he put the idea aside. George would take his mother's side, or simply say he didn't want to be involved.

For the rest of the afternoon he sat at his mother's desk looking at the papers he had stacked up on the floor. Most of them were bills or business letters. There were a few letters from friends, but none of them went back twenty-five years to the time when he was born.

In the drawer where he had found the photo he also found his mother's and stepfather's passports. Then he found their wills, which left everything they had to him.

All this had taken him a couple of hours. By the time he began looking through the photo albums in the front room the day was nearly over. He rang Louise to tell her he would be home soon.

'Why don't you leave it now? You haven't found anything.' She sounded anxious.

'I'll be back soon,' he said.

The photos seemed to be no more help than the papers had been. There were several snapshots of Daniel as a baby. In some of them Sarah was holding him, but there was no sign of Chris, or anyone else who might have been his father.

Daniel put the albums away and stood up, thinking about the final place where he could look.

Somehow he hadn't wanted to look in the chest of drawers in his mum's bedroom where she kept her clothes. He knew she sometimes used to hide things there. In the old days when his birthday was coming up, he always knew where the presents would be, wrapped neatly in birthday paper.

He walked up the stairs slowly. In the bedroom he opened the big bottom drawer and began digging into the neatly folded piles of his mother's underwear, feeling like a thief. The cloth was soft, clinging to his fingertips, and he found himself looking away, not wanting to see his hands touching his mother's bras and pants.

He was about to give up when he struck something hard. Another photo album.

He sat back on the floor next to the chest of drawers and opened it. The first pages were full of wedding pictures. He had a vague memory of seeing these pictures long ago, but now he looked at them as if it was the first time.

At a quick glance the bride looked

like his mum, then he realized that it was his Aunt Nancy. She looked happy and excited. His mum stood beside her in some of the pictures, the same flush of pleasure showing on her face.

Seeing them together like this gave Daniel an odd feeling of sadness. He was now older than they must have been at the time. How much his mother must have missed her sister, he thought. He was an only child so he couldn't imagine what it was like, but he could guess how lonely and sad she must have been when Nancy died.

He looked at the guests in the background of the pictures carefully, but there were no black faces in the crowd. He started to shut the album, then he noticed that the photos on the next page were different. These were photos from the time his mum had graduated from college. There was a big picture of her in a gown and a flat hat holding a scroll. The other pictures were groups of her classmates dressed in the same way. In two of them the black man Brownjohn had called Chris was standing in the middle.

In one photo he had his arm round the girl next to him. In the other photo he had his hat in his hand as if he was going to throw it up in the air. He looked handsome and a little bit reckless, as if he knew he was cool and on top of everything.

'Chris,' Daniel whispered. 'Chris.'

He couldn't guess why his mother had kept it from him, but he felt now that he knew without a shadow of a doubt that this was his father. This was the proof. These pictures were things his mum meant to hide, without a shadow of a doubt. 'Chris,' he whispered again.

Suddenly he felt his eyelids sting and before he could even try to stop it there were tears rolling down his cheeks. 'My dad,' he said, right out loud this time. 'You're my dad.'

CHAPTER NINE

'Nothing's really changed,' Louise told him.

It was close to midnight. Daniel had spent hours, he didn't know how long, walking around. He couldn't call to mind where he had gone or why. He had simply walked until the ache in his legs told him it was time to stop.

In the flat Louise was sitting watching the telly, but she was really waiting for him. 'I'm worried about you,' she said. 'Why don't you just wait and talk to your mum? All this snooping about can't be good. Honest. You haven't found out anything, just upset yourself.'

'No point talking to her,' he replied. 'She'll just tell me the same bollocks she always has. And I *have* found out something. I've seen those pictures she was hiding. What do you think that's all about? Why do you think she was hiding them?'

Louise didn't answer. She didn't know how to reply to those questions.

That was for certain, but she was certain, also, that there was something wrong about the way Daniel was going behind his mum's back. The other thing that worried her was that in one day Daniel had changed. She couldn't put her finger on it, but she felt he was torn by feelings and thoughts about which she knew nothing.

'I don't like it,' she said.

'Tough,' Daniel said before he could stop himself, then saw the hurt look on her face. 'I'm sorry,' he said, 'but why don't you help me, instead of having a go?'

The oddest thing, he reflected, was the way his feelings about Louise had changed. Before this he would have welcomed her support. Now he had the sense that she was afraid or worried, and that her comments were really meant to discourage him. What she wanted, he thought, was to put all this behind them. After that they could carry on living like a nice middle-class couple. There would be nothing to connect them to anything sordid, like a dad who had run off.

Louise changed the subject. There seemed to be no point in taking her doubts further; and while Daniel was at his mother's she had been thinking about the entire riddle. She had some ideas about how to start solving it. 'Have you looked in her computer?' she asked.

'I tried, but I didn't know the password. I never got anywhere.'

'I had an idea when you mentioned that photo of the students getting their degrees. If you checked out the other people in the picture they might be able to tell you something.'

'That would be a good idea if I knew their names or how to find them,' Daniel said sarcastically.

'But you could find out,' Louise said. She smiled at him with a hint of triumph. 'I was looking at our college website. A lot of our old classmates put down their names after uni. They give the place, the names, the dates and what they're doing now. Maybe you can find at least a few of your mum's old friends on her college site.'

Daniel stared at her, wondering why he hadn't thought of it first. 'You're a bloody genius,' he said.

The truth was that he had been stuck for what to do next. When he despatched his class to do what they called research it was all about looking up names and dates which everyone knew. The history he studied had been about making sense of great events and periods of time. He had no experience of looking up certificates of birth and death or addresses. As far as he was concerned that was biography. When it came to tracking down someone who might be alive he had no idea.

They went straight to the computer. Louise hadn't lost her doubts, but now she was involved and she was eager to get on with the job.

They found the website for his mother's old college, went to the graduate section, and started checking the names and dates.

'Anything around 1978,' Daniel said.

In a short while they had a list of people who had got their degrees in the same year and in the same subject as his mother. There were three Christophers on the list, but none of them had a Nigerian surname. There was, in fact, only one name which looked African.

They had a brief debate about which to try first.

'Let's try the Christophers first,' Louise said. 'I don't think it will be one of them, but tracking them down will give you some practice.'

Daniel agreed. He wasn't convinced by what Louise said, but now he was face to face with a chance of finding out he wasn't so sure that he wanted to go through with it. They spent the next couple of hours checking their list in the phone book.

The problem was that these were the sort of names which were repeated several times.

'We could ring them all,' Louise said doubtfully.

In the end they sent an email message to everyone saying that a graduate of that year wanted to get in touch.

'If no one rings in a couple of days,' Daniel said, 'I'll try something else.'

He didn't know what to expect. He asked Louise the same question over and over again. 'Do you think they'll be bothered?'

Louise kept telling him to calm

down, but he fidgeted throughout the next day.

It was like waiting for exam results. On most Sundays they went out, to the movies, or at least a stroll round the park. This time Daniel refused to leave the house, in case the phone rang. The call came late in the evening.

'This is Chris Reilly,' the voice said. 'I saw your message. Who am I speaking to? What's it about?'

He sounded cheerful, as if he thought what was coming would be an invite to a party. Quickly, Daniel told him who he was. 'I'm doing this for my mother. We want to give her a surprise.'

He told Reilly his mother's name and the subject she had studied. There was a long pause.

'I think I know who you mean: slim, blonde? Weren't many like her about, but I didn't really know her. She was one of the feminists, I think. No. I didn't really know her.'

I'm not surprised, Daniel thought. He also thought he already knew the answer to his next question, but he asked it anyway.

'Were there any black students? She mentioned a Nigerian.'

'Oh there were a couple around,' Reilly said, 'but I didn't really know them.'

'Yes. Thank you,' Daniel said, getting ready to put the phone down.

All of a sudden he had the sinking feeling that if he got any more calls they would all be like this.

'Wait a minute,' Reilly said. 'There is someone who might know, a woman who organized a couple of reunions. Jane. She seems to know everyone. I'll find the number for you.'

CHAPTER TEN

Daniel wasted no time in phoning the number Reilly had given him. Jane Davis answered on the first ring, as if she had been waiting for the call. She had a friendly, giggly voice, and Daniel relaxed from the moment he heard her speak.

He told her who he was and repeated his story about giving his mum a surprise.

'Do you know graduates from 1978 I can get in touch with?' he asked.

'1978. 1978,' she said slowly. 'It's a long way before my time, but I know a woman who might know. Kate Hall. She was in your mother's year and she's a teacher too. They would have known each other.'

Daniel rang the number she gave him without delay. At first he was poised to say who he was and to tell his story, but all he heard was the ringing sound. After a while he resigned himself to the fact that there was no answer and he slammed the phone down.

'Try again later,' Louise said.

He sat down, frustrated, and he was just about to tell Louise what Jane Davis had said when the phone rang again. This time it was his mother.

'I see you've been clearing out the shed,' she said. 'That's a good job.'

Her voice was cheerful, and he guessed that she hadn't noticed that he had been searching through her room.

'I want to ask you something, Mum.'

Somehow, she picked up something strange about the tone of his voice. 'What's the matter?'

'It's that photo.' For a moment the urge to tell her that he'd seen the hidden album flashed through his mind. Then he stopped himself. 'I think I've seen it before. Are you sure you don't know who that man is?'

There was a pause, and when she replied her voice sounded curt and snappy. 'I told you as much the other night. Why are you asking again?'

'No reason,' he said, trying to sound casual. 'I just thought I'd ask.'

'All right.' It sounded now as if she was trying to smooth things over. 'Come to dinner on Wednesday. I've got meetings every night till then. Bring Louise. We'll have a proper chat.'

'Louise can't come. She's off to the West Country until next week.' She was taking some time off before the wedding and wanted to stay with her parents to say a proper goodbye to her old life, she had told Daniel. 'I'll try,' he said, doubtfully.

'She's still messing me about,' he told Louise when he'd put the phone down.

'You can ask her Wednesday,' she said.

'What can I ask her? She said it's all a mistake. I don't really know that's not true, except for that photo. That doesn't prove anything. If she's been hiding something my whole life, she's not going to just tell me now.'

'Maybe,' Louise said, 'when you talk to this woman Kate Hall she can tell you something that will help.'

Daniel agreed. Next day he rang the number several times, but there was no reply. It was a bad day, and his failure to reach Kate Hall made him feel even more gloomy. Normally, he could hide his bad moods, but this time he didn't even try. He was at his most depressed during lunchtime and the breaks. His usual habit was to hang out with a group of the younger teachers. Instead, he paced the playground, glaring at anyone who got in his way. He couldn't think about anything except the problem of his father, but there was no one he wanted to tell. Like any other school, Daniel's was a hotbed of gossip. If he told any of his friends, it would be all round the place in a flash and he couldn't stand the thought of everyone talking about him.

His mood was so obvious that his friends simply steered clear of him. No one dared joke about the wedding.

He was clearing up his desk at the end of the day when Judy came up and touched him on the arm. 'You all right?'

'Pretty dreadful, thank you,' he replied.

'If you want to talk,' she said quietly, 'we could go for a drink.'

The softness of her tone made him look round at her. She looked straight back at him. Black hair, light brown eyes. For a moment he felt as if he was seeing her for the first time. He was trying to speak, to say no, but somehow he couldn't get the word out.

'I don't want to pry,' she said quietly, 'but I can see there's something wrong.'

There was something strange about this, he thought. Here he was going through the most painful time of his life so far. Louise was pregnant but the last few days she had put up with his moods without complaint, and now she was waiting for him at home. At the same time, all in one quick look, he had taken in Judy's hair, her eyes and the swell of her breasts. His mind was still full of his trouble, but, in that instant, he could feel his body reacting strongly.

'I . . . I can't,' he stammered.

Judy seemed to move a little closer. 'A few years ago,' she said, 'a couple of years ago, I went through a bad time, and no one noticed. I know what it's like. You're a member of my team. If you want to talk. OK?'

He nodded his consent. 'OK.'

Later on that night he thought about what Judy had said. He had been tempted to tell her. Louise had gone to bed early, and in the hushed silence of the flat Daniel sat turning over the pages of one of the chapters he was about to ask his pupils to read. When it struck him that he ought to ring Kate Hall again, it was already past eleven.

He rang the number anyway. He had decided to put the phone down after it had rung half a dozen times, but on the second ring a woman answered. Taken by surprise, Daniel stumbled over his words, but she listened to what he was telling her without butting in.

'I did know your mum,' she said when he paused for breath. 'How is she?'

'She's fine,' he said. 'She's fine.' He paused again, thinking through what to say. 'I wondered if you could help me locate some of her old friends.'

'I don't know.'

She sounded doubtful. It suddenly struck Daniel that she wouldn't want to answer his questions on the phone. He could be anyone.

'Can I come and see you?' he asked. 'Tomorrow?'

CHAPTER ELEVEN

Daniel spent the day in an anxious, excited frame of mind. What made matters worse was the fact that he didn't know what he was trying to find out.

Was his father alive or not? Was his mother lying, and, if she were, why would she lie?

On his way to work he still couldn't get his mind off the subject; and in the middle of the school day he kept on puzzling over the same questions.

He had given his year group the early part of the day to read a chapter from a classic novel. Later on he would divide them into smaller groups to talk about what they had read. In the meantime he sat in the staff room trying to ready himself for the day ahead. Before leaving home that morning he had decided to make a real effort.

He would be patient. He would smile at his fellow teachers. He would avoid scowling at the school bullies. In other words, he would try to be his normal self.

At lunchtime he went up to Judy and began talking to her about the project.

'You saw Mr Brownjohn?' she asked.

He told her about his visit to the old teacher. 'I thought I would invite him in to talk to the entire class. He's got a lot to say.'

He didn't tell her quite how much. She smiled and nodded as if to show she approved. All this was normal and for a while Daniel almost forgot how much he had fancied her only the day before.

At the end of their talk she

75

lowered her voice again. 'Are you all right now?'

For a few seconds they looked into each other's eyes. The room seemed to go quiet around them.

'Yes. Thanks,' Daniel said.

'I want to talk to you,' she said.

They went into an empty classroom.

'What's the problem?' she asked him.

The problem, he thought, was that all of a sudden he wanted to kiss her and touch her body. Up to a couple of days ago he would have been worried about Louise and how she would feel. Now he didn't seem to care.

'You're feeling trapped, aren't you?' Judy said.

He was about to open his mouth and say that he wasn't when he realized that in the last few days that was exactly how he was feeling.

'Why are you asking me?' he replied.

She shrugged. 'It takes one to know one,' she said.

The door opened and a group of children looked in. A queue had begun to build up along the passage outside.

'Let's talk again,' she said.

It wasn't till later on that he thought about Louise and marriage. Had he wanted her at the start in the way he now wanted Judy? It had been much more relaxed. Sex with Louise had been part of going together. It had been a pleasure he got used to. But it had been easy, part of why he liked her, and it was something they did because they liked each other. Then it had been love—or that was what he thought. He could never imagine, though, pushing Louise up against the wall and pulling her skirt up. This was the exact thought that had come into his mind when he faced Judy in the empty classroom. What would life be like if he had these thoughts all day, then had to go home to Louise?

The rest of the day dragged on and on, but he still couldn't focus as usual. It was a relief when the school day ended and he could leave.

He had arranged to meet Kate Hall at a café in the shopping centre near the school where she taught. The café was a big open space on the first floor of the shopping mall. Kate was sitting alone at a table not far from the entrance to the multiplex cinema. He would have guessed, he thought, that she was a teacher. Somehow he had expected her to look a bit like his mother, but she didn't. She was small and plump. She had iron-grey hair and she was wearing a dark checked skirt, a white blouse and a fawn-coloured raincoat. He went straight up to her table and sat facing her.

'You're Daniel,' she said. She smiled. 'You look like your voice. A lot of people don't. How is your mother?'

He told her his mother was fine and then went on to repeat his story about the surprise he wanted to arrange. In a couple of minutes he could see she had relaxed and was starting to trust him.

'Your mother had a lot of friends,' she said. 'She was good fun.'

'Do you know any of them?'

'It's a long time ago. I'm out of touch now.' She reached down and picked up her briefcase from the floor. 'I've got a couple of pictures here, though. I can tell you who they are.'

Daniel's heart seemed to skip a beat. Perhaps this was it. 'Just what I needed,' he said, trying to sound casual.

The pictures were of the same group. There were a couple of dozen students, lined up in two rows. Kate went through them, pointing with her finger and calling out the names she could recall. 'There's your mother,' she said. 'She was so pretty.'

She sighed. 'What about her sister? I only met her once or twice but she was a beauty.' She lowered her voice. 'I think she got into some kind of trouble. Your mother had to take some time off. But that was a long time ago. How is she now?'

'She died.'

Kate looked shocked, and Daniel hurried to explain that this too was a long time ago. Without leaving her the time to respond, he pointed to the photo. Chris was standing in the second row, almost behind his mother. The features were blurred, not distinct, but Daniel knew who it was right away. 'Who's this?' he asked.

'Oh him. That's Chris. Chris Adebowale.' She said the name with some care, bit by bit, AD DAY BO WA LAY. She smiled with a touch of smugness at Daniel. 'He was quite a lad. I couldn't forget him. There used to be a man on TV from time to time with the same name. They

80

were always getting it wrong, but it stuck with me.'

'Have you ever seen him again?' he asked.

'Oh no,' she said. 'Shame, really. A friend of mine saw him about ten years ago. I've lost touch with her now, but she was at Heathrow going somewhere, and she saw him. Coming towards her, large as life. They spoke. He was on his way to Nigeria. Last I ever heard of him.'

CHAPTER TWELVE

'Well, the problem is that knowing his name doesn't really change anything,' Louise said. 'Just because she kept those photos to herself doesn't have to mean what you think it means. It may just be that it reminded her of something she wanted to keep private.'

'Yeah,' Daniel replied sarcastically.

'Guess what?'

'Women do things that you wouldn't. We keep letters, bits of things which look like rubbish to anyone else but they remind us of something precious that doesn't matter to anyone else.'

'My mum's not that sort of woman,' Daniel said.

The ironic smile that crossed Louise's face was one of the few things he didn't like about her. 'How do you know?'

'I know my own mother.'

'So you know she loves you. She's crazy about you. Why don't you trust her?'

Daniel thought about it. 'I do trust her. It's just that I always felt there was something wrong.' He couldn't find the words to explain to Louise. When he was little he used to have the secret idea that there had been a mistake; that his dad was still alive somewhere, and one day they would meet. Now it all seemed to be coming true.

'A few days ago I didn't know this person existed,' he told Louise. 'Now I have his name and I know what he looks like. Finding him won't be too hard.'

'Suppose he's gone back to Nigeria.'

'Then it won't be easy.' He paused, thinking about it. 'I'll cross that bridge when I come to it.'

They spent the rest of the night working out how to locate Chris. There were a dozen Adebowales in the London phone book, but none of them had the initial C.

'He needn't be here,' Louise said. 'He could be anywhere in the country.'

By the time they went to bed Daniel had run out of ideas.

In the morning Louise packed her suitcase early, and Daniel put it in the boot of the car. He had arranged his classes so he could go in halfway through the morning. This gave them time to talk before Louise left to drive down to Devon.

'Should I stay?' she asked at the last moment. 'I can put it off.'

Daniel shook his head firmly. He didn't want to say it, but he wanted to be alone. Louise's absence would give him the chance to think through what to do.

By lunchtime he had only decided one thing. He couldn't face his mother that evening. He was too upset and angry not to talk about the photos. On the other hand, if she had a simple answer he would look stupid. He would have to admit that he had searched through her things behind her back and just thinking about that made Daniel feel hot with shame.

Before he could change his mind he phoned her house and left a message saying he was busy. That gave him time, he thought, to sort the mess out once and for all. Later on that night he phoned Jane Davis again. He had a name to give her now. She might have come across Chris at one of her reunions. Perhaps there were lists of old students which might help him. In any case, he couldn't think of what else to do.

'How is it going?' she asked. 'I was wondering if you'd managed to locate the people you wanted. Be good if you could tell them about the website. Did you ring Kate?'

Daniel forced himself to reply. He had to make an effort to sound casual, and he hardly knew what he was saying. 'There is one name you could help me with,' he said, 'Chris Adebowale.'

'Chris what?'

He repeated the name slowly.

'That's funny,' she said. 'I was looking through some of the names that came up. I can't find that name, but I was once in touch with an African guy from that year.'

The line went silent, and for a moment Daniel thought they'd been cut off. 'Hello,' he said.

'I'm still here.' Jane replied. 'I was trying to think. This guy lectures at one of the London colleges. I ran into him at a meeting, and it turned out we had studied at the same place. He was asking about his year too. I've got his card somewhere.'

'What's his name?'

'I don't have the first idea. I'll have to dig it out. Give me a while. I'll ring you back.'

Daniel waited by the phone for another ten minutes. Then he sat down and tried to read. Giving that up, he tried watching the news on TV, but the words he was hearing seemed to make no sense. In the end he simply sat back on the sofa and gazed at the wall. The phone didn't ring until almost two hours later.

'Sorry,' Jane Davis said. 'I meant to ring you before, but I had a couple of calls.'

'That's all right,' Daniel said.

If only she knew, he thought, how

hard the waiting had been.

'I found the card,' Jane said brightly. 'His name is Femi Oladapo.'

Daniel had been holding his breath, hoping that it would be Chris. Now his sense of being let down was so strong he could hardly speak.

Jane didn't stop there. She gave him the name and phone number of the college where Femi worked. 'No point ringing now,' she said. She giggled. 'I expect he'll have gone home.'

'Is there any point ringing at all?' Daniel asked. 'It didn't sound as if he knew much more than you.'

Jane's voice took on a note of surprise. Hearing it, Daniel cursed himself for being so careless. She had no idea about his real motives. 'I thought,' she said, 'you wanted to get in touch with people from that year.'

'I do,' Daniel replied. 'Thank you. I'll call him.'

'Of course I thought, being

African, he might be in touch with the other chap.'

'Yes,' Daniel said, but all of a sudden his patience was running out. He didn't want to put her back up, but the thought that she believed all black people would know each other annoyed him. 'You think they'll know each other because they're both African?'

'Maybe,' Jane replied. She sounded cooler and a little more distant. 'There were a few black girls in my year and I didn't think they would, but they all kept in touch. You'd be surprised.'

Thinking about it later on, Daniel guessed that what Jane had said made sense. Somehow he felt that he was about to set foot on the right track. The truth couldn't be far away.

CHAPTER THIRTEEN

At school the next day Daniel took the first chance he had to ring Femi. He got a switchboard which put him through to Femi's phone, but the only answer he got was a machine. As the morning wore on, he tried again a couple of times with the same result. It wasn't until a few minutes before the end of his lunch break that he was answered by a voice on the other end of the line.

'Femi Oladapo.'

Daniel told him who he was and that he was trying to locate his mother's classmates.

'Oh yes,' Femi said. 'I knew her. You want me to come to a party or something?'

'That's right,' Daniel said. After all this, he thought, he'd have to organize something. 'Do you happen to know how to get in touch with

Chris Adebowale?'

The line went silent, and Daniel repeated the name.

'I don't think so,' Femi said slowly. 'I don't know who you mean.'

Daniel's stomach churned. For a moment it felt as if he was going down in a fast lift. 'But he was in the same class.'

'Was he? I don't recall the name.'

'He was an African from Nigeria.'

The instant Daniel said that he wished he could call it back. When Femi replied, his voice seemed to have lost its warmth. 'Yes, well, we don't all know each other.'

Daniel stammered, trying to find the words to explain.

'I'm sorry,' Femi said. 'I have to go now. Let me know if you want me to come to the party. I'd like to.'

The phone went dead. Daniel stood in the corner as his fellow teachers went by, streaming back to their classes. He was sure that the way Femi reacted showed he was hiding something. Until Daniel said Chris's name he had been friendly and open. Then he had shut down.

Lost in his own thoughts Daniel didn't notice that Judy had come up and was speaking to him. She had said something about a meeting.

'A meeting?'

'That's right,' Judy said. 'I sent you all an email. Today at four o'clock.'

'I can't come,' Daniel said.

Up to that point he hadn't decided, but as he spoke he knew what he had to do later. Femi was hiding something and he couldn't get him to reveal it on the phone. Perhaps Femi had assumed that he was a white person when they spoke. When they met face to face he might be more willing to help. He had to go and see him. If he went right away he might just be in time. He knew that college lecturers had more flexible times. Today he knew where to find Femi. Tomorrow the man might be somewhere else.

Judy was frowning and he tried to soften his tone.

'Sorry. Some family business.' He knew it sounded lame, but it was all he could think of at short notice.

Judy looked at him and sighed. 'Of course, I forgot the wedding. All right, but don't blame me if you get landed with all the crap jobs.'

Daniel shrugged and Judy frowned again. 'Your mind's somewhere else, isn't it?'

Daniel shrugged again. He knew she was finding his manner strange, unlike his usual style, but he couldn't be bothered to explain.

'Got your mobile?' she asked suddenly.

'Yes.'

'Get it out. Show it to me.'

She gestured, and he took the mobile out of his pocket. 'Put this number on the speed dial. It's my home number. If there's a problem tomorrow, ring and let me know.'

'I'll be here,' he protested, but he

tapped the number in.

At the end of the day, Daniel ran out of the school gates as quickly as he could. Femi's college was across the river in South London near Elephant and Castle, so he didn't get there until it was close to five o'clock.

At the desk in the lobby he asked for Femi. The woman sitting there asked for his name in return, then she ran her finger down a list pinned to her clipboard. 'Does he expect you?'

'I'm not sure.'

He didn't want to risk saying no, but he didn't want to tell her an outright lie.

She gazed at him, her eyes running over him from head to toe. She must have decided he was harmless, because she picked up the phone and spoke briefly. Then she turned to look at him again. 'What is it about?'

'It's about a conference,' Daniel said, taking a wild guess.

She spoke again, then she put the phone down and said Mr Oladapo would be down in a couple of minutes. Daniel waited by the turnstile. Beyond it was a marble staircase where a stream of students were coming and going. In a few minutes Daniel saw a short, bulky black man with a shiny round face walking down. Femi. He was smiling at the students, but when he saw Daniel his face went blank.

'What can I do for you?' he asked, his tone almost abrupt.

'We talked on the phone,' Daniel said.

'Ah. I thought I'd heard the name before.' He paused, looking straight at Daniel. 'I told you all I know on the phone. I can't help you any more.'

'I know this seems a bit strange,' Daniel said, 'but I have a good reason for this.'

He took the photo Brownjohn had lent him out of his pocket and handed it to Femi. 'That's him, isn't it? And that's my mother.'

Femi held the photo in front of him, looking at it. He was smiling a little. Looking at his face now, Daniel knew for certain that he knew both the people in the photo. His smile said that he was thinking of the old days.

'That baby,' Femi said. 'Would that be you?'

Daniel nodded.

'I saw Chris not so long ago,' Femi told him. He was still gazing at the photo. 'It's just that I didn't know who you were.'

CHAPTER FOURTEEN

The floor seemed to lurch below Daniel's feet. Chris, the man who might be his father, was alive. Femi had seen him. He would know where to find him.

95

'He's alive,' Daniel said. 'He's alive?'

Femi gave him a puzzled look. 'Yes, of course. Well, he was alive when I saw him about a year ago. We talked.'

'You said you didn't know who he was.'

Femi laughed. 'Did I say that?'

Daniel didn't answer.

Femi gestured, waggling his fingers. 'It's just that he said not to talk about seeing him. At the time it didn't matter. I had no idea someone might ask.'

Daniel's heart sank. 'Why? Is he in some kind of trouble?'

'No. I don't think so. It was something to do with his business. I don't know. He didn't really give me any details. I expect it's all blown over now.'

'What does he do?'

'Some kind of import–export thing.' He paused, crinkling up his forehead in thought. 'Wait a minute.

He gave me a card with his business address.' He tapped his forehead. 'Oh, I forget what it was, but I've got the card somewhere. Maybe in my office.' He looked at Daniel, his eyes intent and serious. 'Why is this so important?'

Daniel fumbled for the right answer. 'There's no point in putting this party on if I miss out my mum's best friends, is there?'

Femi nodded as if he was convinced. 'OK,' he said. 'Hang on.'

He turned around, went through the turnstile and vanished up the stairs. Daniel waited, his eyes fixed on the top of the staircase. Femi was only gone for a few minutes, but it seemed like an age. When Daniel saw him coming back he let out his breath. He seemed to have been holding it for a while.

Femi held out a card. Daniel read it in one quick glance. It was the right name—*Chris Adebowale*, and printed under it was the name of the firm—*Adepo Imports.* Below that was the address of an industrial estate in Tottenham.

'Thank you,' Daniel said. He felt like hugging Femi. 'Thanks a lot.'

It was past six when he left Femi's college. By this time offices would already be closed. It was much too late to go running over to Tottenham. He walked north towards the river. Once there he crossed a bridge and leaned over to look at the muddy water. Behind him the lights of the London Eye wavered slowly through the air. He walked away from them strolling towards Tower Bridge.

The last time he had walked here was with his mother. Thinking about her made him realize what he was doing. Dawdling by the river was an escape, he thought. Standing there, he wouldn't have to think about what to do next. He wouldn't have to think, either, about meeting his father. If he was honest with himself the idea frightened him.

What could he say to the man? Perhaps he could tell him how much he had missed having a real dad. Perhaps he could ask about his mum. He could ask why he had left, and why she had kept the truth hidden. Perhaps, he thought, it was all his mum's fault. Perhaps she had been cold and distant, the way she was sometimes. He didn't believe everything he had ever read or heard about Africans. He was half an African himself, but he had begun to think of Chris as hot blooded, full of laughter and passion. So much about his mum was cool and formal. Maybe she had put him off.

Looking up he realized that he had walked a long way. He was now somewhere near Canary Wharf. All of a sudden it struck him that he was tired. The night before he had been restless, his mind full of confused thoughts. He had only managed a couple of hours' sleep. Sitting on a bench looking across at the giant cliffs of concrete, he phoned Louise. She answered quickly, as if she'd been waiting. 'I phoned home,' she said. 'I thought maybe you'd gone to see your mum.'

He told her about Femi, and her voice took on a worried tone.

'Shall I come back?'

'No. I'll be OK. I'll call you tomorrow and tell you how I got on.'

He already had the plan in his head. Next day he would go to the industrial park and talk to Chris. Thinking about it, he realized that going after school might be too late. He rang the number Judy had given him earlier.

'We missed your wise counsel today,' she said, 'but you did get a couple of horrible little jobs. That will slow you down when you come back.'

Daniel ignored the banter. 'I need to get off at lunchtime,' he replied.

The sound of her tongue clicking

told him she was annoyed. 'OK, Daniel. I'm giving you some space, but don't do this too often.'

'I'm sorry,' Daniel said. 'I've got to sort something out.'

'Why don't we have a talk tomorrow?'

It's none of her business, he thought. His next thought was that things might get awkward if he upset her. 'I'll need to get away quickly tomorrow,' he said. ' I'll tell you what I can as soon as this gets sorted.'

He put the phone back in his pocket and stayed sitting on the bench, too tired to move. Tomorrow, he thought. I'll see Chris tomorrow and I'll know all I ever wanted to know.

'Tomorrow,' he muttered aloud to himself. 'Tomorrow.'

CHAPTER FIFTEEN

When Daniel went to bed he felt as if he would sleep for days. Instead, he was awake in a couple of hours, and he stayed awake. By the time he set off for school he felt drained of energy, in the mood to go back to bed. To make matters worse he felt anxious and fearful about what he had to do later.

He was just about to leave when the doorbell rang. Postman, he thought, but when he opened the door it was his stepfather, George, standing there.

'Can I come in?'

'I'm just off to school.'

'Just a few minutes.'

He stepped aside and followed George into the flat. His stepfather had never visited, and Daniel could hardly hide his surprise. On the other hand, he guessed right away that it was something to do with his real father.

'It's about your dad,' George said. 'Your mother's had a couple of calls. She's worried about you.'

'Why doesn't she tell me that herself?' Daniel asked.

George shrugged.'It's tricky. There are lots of things she doesn't want to talk about.' He paused. 'Even to me.'

'Do you know whether he's alive?' Daniel asked him. 'And where he is?'

'Look,' George said. 'I don't know any more than you do. What I wanted to tell you was that your mother's upset.'

'I've upset her before. You never said anything.'

George sighed. 'That was different. But these phone calls. She got a call from a woman who said you were asking about your father. Then she got a couple of calls she wouldn't tell me about. I think they must have been from the same man. She told him not to call again, but he did. Then she told me she's changing the number. She said it was some guy she had fallen out with. It appears that he stalked her once, and now he's starting again.'

'You don't believe that.'

'I don't know what to think,' George said. 'But I have the feeling it's all about what you're doing.'

'I'm just trying to see if I can find out about my dad,' Daniel said. 'I always thought he was dead, or I would have done it before. Now there's some mystery. I want to know what it is.'

At the door, as George left, he shook Daniel's hand. The gesture touched Daniel. Looking at George walking down the path it struck him that his stepfather somehow cared more about him than he had imagined. For a moment he thought about calling him back, but George didn't turn around and the moment passed.

Within half an hour Daniel was at

work. During the morning he avoided Judy. He wasn't sure now about how to respond to her offers of help. His life had been simple only a few days before. Now it was a complete muddle.

He reached the industrial estate after two o'clock. The entrance was not far from a tube station, but the site was larger than Daniel expected. It took him nearly half an hour of tramping around before he found the correct unit.

Adepo Imports was on the second floor of a three-storey block. Daniel climbed the stairs, followed the sign which read *Reception* and found himself in a small, neat lobby. It contained three chairs, two tall plants, and a desk where a young black woman sat in front of a computer screen. 'Can I help you?' she asked, barely glancing at Daniel.

He asked for Mr Adebowale.

'He's not here right now. What is it about?'

'It's a private matter,' he told her.

She swivelled round in her chair to look at him. She was wearing a wig with long bronze-coloured dreadlocks. They swung about her face when she turned. 'He's not here,' she repeated.

'Can I wait? How long do you think he'll be?' He gestured at the chairs.

'No point,' the woman said. 'I don't know when he'll be back.'

It struck Daniel that the idea of his waiting around disturbed her. 'I don't mind,' he said. 'What time do you close?'

'Five o'clock.'

'So he should be back by then.'

'I don't know. He may have meetings. It's not a good idea to wait.'

There was a distinct tension in her voice. Daniel wrote his name, address and phone number on a sheet of paper and gave it to her.

'What's this?'

'Can you give it to him?'

'Leave it there,' she said.

He dropped it on the desk and walked away, down the stairs. As he went he thought he could feel her eyes on his back.

Once outside he thought about what to do. If Chris was not in the building, there was nothing he could do about it. He decided to go away and come back later but changed his mind as he reached the entrance to the estate, and decided to wait. There was only one road in, and there was a bus stop across the street close by. The stop had a shelter and was close enough for him to see the cars going in and out. Daniel waited on the bench.

A couple of hours passed. Daniel hardly took his eyes off the turning. He was also trying to see through the windows of every car going in and that was harder than he had thought it would be. Sometimes there was a bus in the way when a car went past.

Sometimes there were two or three cars in a row and he missed one. Half a dozen or more had black drivers, but none looked like Chris. He was on the verge of giving up several times, but somehow he couldn't. If he didn't find out now, he kept thinking, he might never know. Staring at the cars across the road he willed himself to believe. Sooner or later one of them would contain Chris.

He gave it until about a quarter of an hour before five. Then he crossed the road and walked back. As he got closer to Adepo Imports his heart skipped a beat.

Parked outside the building was a black Mercedes. It hadn't been there before.

As soon as he saw it, Daniel knew. He had no idea how he knew, but he was certain the car belonged to Chris.

Instead of going in he stood outside. He leaned against the wall

108

where he couldn't be seen from the windows and waited. In a few minutes the young woman he had seen in the office came out. She glanced at him, almost halting in her stride. Then she walked on, fishing in her purse. In a moment he saw her take out a mobile phone and hold it to her ear.

Nothing happened for a while. He had expected Chris to follow the woman out, but no one appeared. For the next half an hour there was much movement up and down the road, cars pulling out and returning home as the offices closed. The lights went out on the ground floor of the Adepo building. A white man came out and walked over to a car parked across the road. By six o'clock the site was silent, with only the occasional car rolling past.

The lights were still glowing on the second floor of the building. Daniel went over to the door and pushed, but it was locked. He rang the bell, but there was no reply. It was still light, but the site was growing shadowy as the sun dipped below the skyline. Around Daniel the shadows grew darker as he watched the Mercedes.

It was almost seven when he heard a sound from inside the building. The lights had gone out on the second floor. In a few seconds the door opened and Chris appeared. He was older and smaller than he appeared in the photos, but Daniel knew him right away.

'Hello,' he called out. 'Mister Adebowale. Excuse me.'

Chris turned and looked at him, his face blank. 'What do you want?' he asked.

'I was waiting for you,' Daniel said.

'So?' He had a deep voice, a precise, almost bossy sound.

'I'm Sarah Harvey's son,' Daniel said. 'You were students in the same class.'

Chris frowned, staring at him as if

trying to make out something he would know about his features. 'Sarah Harvey,' he said slowly. He nodded. 'Yes . . . Sarah.' Then his frown deepened. 'So? What can I do for you?' He kept staring at Daniel, waiting for an answer.

Daniel was tongue-tied, searching through his brain for the words he wanted to say. They stood like this, both silent, staring at each other for several seconds.

Suddenly, Chris shrugged and gestured with his hands, smiling with a kind of contempt, as if he knew he was dealing with an idiot. 'Sorry,' he said. 'I don't have time for this.'

The car beeped and the lights flashed. He opened the door and got in. Daniel watched him, willing himself to speak. 'I think you're my father,' he blurted out

Chris settled himself in the car and slammed the door. For a moment Daniel thought he hadn't heard, then the driver's window wound down with a slight whine. 'How old are you?' Chris asked in a normal tone of voice, as if they had been talking quietly for hours.

'Twenty-six.'

The engine of the Mercedes purred quietly into life. Chris looked through the window at him. 'You said you're Sarah's son?'

'Yes,' Daniel replied eagerly. 'Yes.'

'Fuck off,' Chris said. 'Fuck off.'

Then he put the car in gear and drove away.

CHAPTER SIXTEEN

Dumbstruck, Daniel watched as the red lights of the car vanished into the half darkness of the estate. He kept hearing the echo of the voice in his ear. It had been the last response he expected, yet, somehow, it was the reaction he had most feared.

Chris couldn't be his father, he

thought. His father would never do that to him. Never. But if this man was his father, the way he acted would explain a lot.

He began walking slowly. He was trying to think, to replay things in his mind—the look on Chris's face, the tone of his voice—but there was only a muddle in his head. He couldn't focus on anything. At the same time he felt tears running down his face. 'Mum,' he said aloud, hearing his own voice like an echo of his thoughts.

He took out his mobile to ring. Before he could press the button a light flashed behind him. At first he thought it was something to do with what he was feeling. He blinked, clearing his eyes. He wiped his face, then he realized that the flashing light came from the headlamps of a car behind him. He turned around to face it, and the car pulled up in front of him.

Two black men got out. They were

big. Daniel was six feet tall, but both of these men were taller and wider. 'What's your game?' one of them said roughly.

They were standing on either side of him and Daniel had a sudden feeling of alarm. It was fully dark now, and there were no cars going past. The entrance to the estate was several hundred metres away. There was no one to see what was going on.

'I'm going home,' Daniel said.

The man laughed. 'You shoulda gone home a long time ago, mate,' he said. 'What's your game?'

At first Daniel had taken them for some kind of private security. Now he wasn't so sure. 'I don't know what you're talking about,' he said. 'Just leave me alone.'

'We've had enough of this,' the man said. 'You scratch one car and you're fucked.'

It hit Daniel then that they took him for some kind of vandal. The thought made him want to laugh.

'You're making a mistake,' he said. 'All right? Goodnight.'

At the same time he started to push past the man who was blocking his way. After that, it was all over in a second. The man's bulk was hard and solid. As Daniel pushed, the man behind caught him round the shoulders and threw him against the car. Daniel twisted round, his hands up in a reflex of self-defence. One of the men punched him in the face and he went down. As he scrambled up on his hands and knees, someone kicked him in the ribs. He went down again. 'Stay away from here,' a voice said in his ear.

Daniel didn't pass out, but he remained lying on the pavement, trying to catch his breath. When he could move again, he sat up, hunching over in an effort to ease the pain. Slowly, he tested his limbs: nothing broken, but his face hurt. The skin felt tight and painful. One eye seemed to be closing and he could feel it swelling. He tried to stand up, but he was so dizzy that he had to sit down again. He looked around. There was no one in sight. It was as if he was in the middle of nowhere.

He fumbled for his phone. Ringing his mother was out of the question, he thought, and Louise was away. There was no one else who would come and pick him up without questions. He ran through his friends in his mind. He didn't want any of them to know about this. At the last moment he thought of Judy. She would come. Strangely enough, the thought of her knowing didn't worry him.

He rang her number and she answered on the first ring.

'I need some help,' he told her. 'Can you come and pick me up?'

She lived nearby and she arrived in about twenty minutes. She was cruising slowly along. He tried to get up but it hurt too much. He sat down again, but her headlights picked him out, and the car stopped. She got out, put her arms round him and helped him to stand. Then she levered him into the front seat next to her.

'Are you all right?' she kept asking. 'Were you mugged? Do you want to go to hospital? Shall I call the police?'

Daniel said no to all except the first question.

'I'm taking you back to my house,' Judy said firmly. 'Then I can take a good look at you.'

Daniel simply nodded his head. From the moment Judy turned up he had given up control, glad to have someone else decide. In the car she glanced sideways at him. 'What happened? What were you doing there?'

'It's a long story.'

'You're not going anywhere,' she said.

Slowly, he told her about the last

few days, starting with his visit to the old teacher, Brownjohn. While he talked they arrived in front of her house. She parked and switched off the engine, still absorbed in his story. When he got to Chris, and what he had said, she drew in her breath sharply. 'You think he sent those men?' she asked.

'I don't know,' Daniel said.

'He can't be your father,' she said. 'If he was he wouldn't do that. Believe me. He wouldn't.'

'I don't know,' Daniel repeated.

She was about to say something else, but hearing the fatigue in his voice she stopped. 'Come on,' she said. 'Let's get you inside.'

She had lived in the house with her husband. Now he was gone she lived alone.

'You can stay in the spare room,' she said.

'I'll go home in a bit,' he told her.

'You need to lie down,' Judy replied. She helped him up the stairs, and into a small bedroom. 'Get undressed and get into bed,' she said. 'Your face needs cleaning up. I'll get something.'

He did what he was told. He was lying in bed, the duvet drawn up to his chin, when she came back. She sat beside him on the bed and began swabbing his face with disinfectant. 'Your eye's almost closed,' she said. 'Maybe we should have gone to the hospital.'

He shook his head. 'No, I'm OK.'

'Why do you think they would do that?' she asked.

Up to that moment Daniel had felt numb, like a puppet on a string. Hearing the question he had, for the first time, a sudden feeling of rage. 'You keep asking that. I don't bloody know,' he snapped at Judy. 'I don't know why any of this happened.'

She made no answer. Instead she took his chin in one hand, and began drying his face with the cotton wool. He looked at her with his good eye.

In the last hour, he realized, he hadn't really looked at her. She was still dressed to go out, in a short denim skirt and a white shirt. She wasn't wearing a bra, and as she bent over him he could see her breasts moving under the shirt.

'Sorry,' he muttered. 'This isn't your fault.'

'Stupid question,' she said briefly. She pulled at the duvet, drawing it back. 'I'm going to look at your chest.'

The bruise was a deep red under his skin.

'This looks nasty,' Judy said. 'Does it hurt.'

'Yes.'

She touched him gently over the bruise, stroking some kind of cream into his skin. Daniel closed his eyes. In his mind was a feeling of surprise about the fact that, tired and injured as he was, his penis was erect. Stiff as a board, he thought.

He felt Judy's hand pause and

move slowly down over his stomach. Then he felt her touching him lower and lower. He reached out and pulled her down towards him. They kissed, gently at first, a long touch of lips. Then her mouth opened over his. Her hand curled around his penis, cuddling it gently.

She got up off the bed, and moved away. The sudden sense of loss made him gasp. He didn't speak. He didn't have the strength, and he didn't, in any case, know what to say.

The light went out and he felt Judy come back and get under the duvet next to him. She must have taken her clothes off because he could feel her cool skin against him from top to toe. He turned and put his arms around her.

'Kiss me again,' she whispered. 'Kiss me.'

CHAPTER SEVENTEEN

In the morning Judy brought him a cup of tea and he woke up long enough to thank her, then went back to sleep. He didn't wake again until hours later.

Through a chink in the curtains he could see that it was a bright, sunny day.

He lay back against the pillows, feeling rested and idle. He still ached all over, but he hardly felt the pain now unless he moved. He looked at the clock, and saw it was past noon. The anger of his meeting with Chris came flooding back. And Louise— she would have phoned last night, he thought. What would he tell her?

He crawled out of bed and dressed, his movements slow and painful. Downstairs, Judy was in the kitchen, sitting at the table drinking coffee. The papers were spread out in front of her. She looked round when he came in and got up.

'I didn't wake you. You looked dead to the world.'

'I have to get back,' he said.

'I'll take you.' Her tone was matter-of-fact and calm, as if this was any morning in the staff room. 'You have time for some breakfast. Sit down.'

While he ate toast, Judy chatted about the weather and the traffic and the headlines in the paper. It was as if the night before had been a dream, except for the fact that he was sitting at her kitchen table.

'What are you going to do about your father and all the rest of it?' Judy asked suddenly.

Daniel had thought about it, but the question still came as a slight shock. 'I don't know,' he admitted.

In the car going back Judy kept up a friendly chatter about nothing very much.

When they stopped in front of his

flat, she turned and put her hand on his arm.

'About last night,' she said. 'It didn't happen, OK?'

'OK,' Daniel replied.

'We can talk when you've sorted yourself out.' She leant over to kiss him on the cheek. 'Good luck.'

Daniel hadn't wanted to talk about what had happened in any case. The strange thing was that he had expected to feel guilty. Instead, thinking about Judy's body, he felt pure delight. He had *wanted* this to happen. It was as if he had taken a step forward which would cut him off from his old life. After this Louise would only bore him. He put to one side what he would say to her or what he would do about the wedding.

In the flat, Daniel went straight to the phone. There were several messages on the machine, most of them from Louise. The last one from the night before said that if she hadn't heard from him by midnight, she would come back in the morning. The next one said that she was on her way. The final message was from his mother. It said that she had to speak to him urgently.

When he rang the bell at his mother's house, George opened the door. First, he exclaimed over Daniel's bruises, then he said that his mother was out.

'What happened?' he asked Daniel.

'I went to see someone I thought could tell me about my dad,' Daniel told him. 'His friends beat me up.'

'Why?'

'You tell me,' Daniel said angrily. 'He was the man in the photo. Chris.'

'Chris?' George stared at him. 'He rang again this morning. He left a number.'

Daniel couldn't make sense of anything; the thought made him feel sick.

'I'm going to phone him,' George said, sounding firm and decided.

'What for?'

'I want to know why he did this to you,' George said. 'Whoever he is, it's not right.'

For a moment Daniel felt like laughing.

'See *what* he did to me, George?'

'Exactly.'

An idea sprang into Daniel's mind. 'What time is my mum getting back?'

'In about an hour. She's at the library.'

'Invite him over,' Daniel said.

'No. I couldn't do that to your mum,' George said, firmly.

'Have you asked her about all this?'

George nodded.

'Did she tell you anything?'

'No.'

'If mum's in trouble I want to know why and how I can help,' Daniel said. 'And so do you. I don't want to mess about. If she's scared of this guy or he's a stalker or something, let's have it out in the open, then we can decide what to do.'

'It's going behind her back,' George said.

'How do you think I feel?' Daniel said. 'She's been going behind my back all the time!'

'I know you *think* that,' George said slowly.

'Please—see what happens. Then, if you want, you can go to the library and tell her what's going on. Maybe that way we'll sort it out. If she won't come, no harm done. I'll get Chris to leave. But if you won't do it, I will. All you have to do is tell my mum about it and see if she wants to see him.'

CHAPTER EIGHTEEN

Louise came over as soon as he called. She was beaming until she saw his face when he answered the door. Then she drew back in alarm.

'What happened to your face? Why are we at your mum's place?'

He told her quickly. Looking at her horrified reaction, it struck him for the first time that there might be some danger in the meeting he had arranged with Chris.

'He's coming here,' he told her.

'What?'

He told her the rest. He ought to be talking to her, he thought, about the wedding and about stopping it all but he couldn't bring himself to do that yet.

'Perhaps you'd better go home,' he said, hoping that she would.

'Of course not,' she said. 'I'm going to stay with you.'

Before he could argue with her the doorbell rang. When he opened the door, Chris was standing there. Seeing Daniel, he frowned a little, as if he was less than happy to see a stranger in front of him.

'I'm looking for Sarah Benson,' he

128

said. He seemed to take another look at Daniel, his forehead creasing up in thought. Then his eyebrows went up in surprise. 'You came to my office last night,' he said.

'You noticed,' Daniel said. 'Should I tell *you* to fuck off?'

Chris smiled. 'Sorry about that,' he said. 'It was a bad moment. I heard about what happened. It was all a mistake.'

'These guys go around beating up anyone who talks to you by mistake?'

Chris shook his head and laughed. 'No. It's just business. I'm into imports and exports. I imported animals a while back. For research.' He saw the puzzled look on Daniel's face. 'They were chimps. I had a contract with some research labs. I got targeted by the animal liberation campaign. They put my name on a website. People poured acid on my car. My windows got broken. I got death threats. So I have a lot of security looking after me. Things just got out of hand.'

'So it was just a mistake.' Louise had come up behind Daniel. Her voice sounded pleased, full of relief.

Daniel knew how she felt. It really had been a mistake. 'OK,' he said. 'That is no problem. But why did you tell me to . . .' he stumbled over the words, 'to fuck off?'

'I didn't know who you were,' Chris said. 'They try all sorts of tricks. Honest. I've had over a year of it. When you said you were twenty-six I figured that you couldn't be Sarah's son. But there were two or three Sarahs, and maybe I mixed them up. The one I was thinking of didn't have a baby twenty-six years ago.'

'Why are you lying?' Daniel burst out. The words had seemed to trigger all his rage. He reached into the pocket of his jacket and took out the photo he had carried for the last few days. He held it up in front of Chris. 'What's this? Who's this supposed to be? You and my mum.'

Chris took the photo without comment and gazed at it for a few seconds. Then he looked up at Daniel. 'That's not Sarah,' he said. 'That's her sister Nancy. We were good friends.'

Daniel stared back at him. For a moment he couldn't make sense of what Chris had said. 'But you are my dad?'

Chris smiled. He shook his head.

'No, really—at the relevant time, I was out of the country. I didn't even know you existed till last night.'

Daniel pointed at the photo again.'So why are you holding me?'

Chris took another look.'That's not Sarah's son. It's her sister Nancy's.'

That was the moment that his mother and George appeared at the gate. His mother's walk seemed even more upright than usual. Her shoulders were held straight back. When she came in, her face didn't

131

react to seeing Chris. Daniel didn't waste any time in showing her the photo.

'What about this, Mum?' He pointed at Chris. 'He says it's not me.'

His mother sighed and looked at Chris. 'This is why I never answered your calls,' she said. 'You don't know what you're talking about. You weren't there. You're making a big mistake.'

She looked directly at Daniel for the first time. 'What happened to your face?' She got up and held his chin to take a good look, but he turned away.

'It's a long story, Mum,' he said. 'I'm all right. What I want to know about is this guy. Why didn't you want to talk to him?'

'I didn't want him to tell you this,' she said. 'Your father's dead. There's no point in trying to find out more. There's no mystery. You go asking people about it and they're confused.

132

They confuse you even more. Why didn't you just ask me?'

Daniel's head was spinning. This was what she'd always said, and he felt the way he used to do as a little boy—that there was something more behind her words, something he would never know. After all he had wished for during the last few days, nothing had changed. 'Why didn't you tell me about knowing Chris?'

For a moment she made no answer.

'Tell him,' George said suddenly. 'This has gone far enough. Whatever it is, he's got a right to know.'

His mother's eyes flickered sideways. 'Don't, George,' she said. 'Just don't.'

'I mean it,' George said. 'I said I'd come to help, but if that's it, let's go right now.'

All of a sudden there were tears in Sarah's eyes. Her face twisted and she began to cry. George bent down and put his arms round her. He whispered something and Sarah looked up and wiped her eyes. 'It was stupid to lie about Chris,' she said. 'I just didn't know what he would say if you found him.'

'What could I say?' Chris asked her.

'You've already said it.' She stared at Daniel as if she was trying to send him a message with her eyes. 'The thing is, I'm not your natural mother. You were my sister Nancy's baby.'

Daniel was speechless. The entire room seemed to be holding its breath.

'Nancy was pregnant when she got married,' Sarah said. 'There was a good chance that it wasn't her husband's, but she didn't think it would matter.'

'But my birth certificate,' Daniel stammered. 'You were my mum.'

Sarah smiled.

'Nancy registered herself as me. She had my passport, but she was confused at the time. Somehow she thought it would protect her husband. She just made up all the details, including the father. I don't know who helped her. I only knew this after.'

'Why didn't you just tell me?' Daniel broke in. 'Does that mean my dad's still alive?'

'It means,' Sarah said harshly, 'that I don't know who your father is. Nancy was pissed one night and she had it off with three blokes on the trot.' She stretched out her hands towards him, pleading. 'Can you see why I didn't want to tell you?'

Daniel didn't answer. In any case he couldn't think of anything to say. The ground seemed to be slipping away beneath his feet.

'Then you turned up,' Sarah went on. 'A black baby. It wasn't fashionable in those days.' She made a sound halfway between a sob and a laugh. 'Two of the guys were black. She didn't know which one it was, didn't even know their names. Her husband said he would stick by her, but his family hated it, and he wasn't able or willing to stand up for her. Chris was a big pal of hers. He used to meet her here because her friends weren't really welcome in her husband's house. She went a bit crazy. She used to leave you with me when she went out. One day she didn't come back.'

Daniel felt a tear trickling down his face, but he didn't bother to wipe it off. 'Why didn't you tell me?'

'I don't know. I should have. When Nancy had her accident I was looking after you. Her husband didn't want you and he didn't object to me keeping you. It seemed so natural. The first time you spoke you called me "Mum". I didn't want to tell you all this stuff. It seemed better at the time. You were mine and I loved you so much. I'm sorry. You're still Daniel. That was the name I gave you.'

Daniel got up and walked over to the window. He stood looking out at the garden. It was as if he'd always known that he wasn't really who he thought he was. In the moment when his mother told him her secret he had felt a stab of grief and loss. Minutes later most of what he felt was relief. It was as if a door had opened up into another world. If he wasn't who he thought he was, Daniel thought, he could be who he wanted to be.

'Your sister,' he heard Louise saying. 'She was your real sister?'

'Yes,' his mother replied. 'She was. Of course she was.'

'Well, that's all right,' Louise said. 'Your DNA will be nearly the same.'

'Yes.'

'Good,' she said. Her tone was pleased, as if all this was the most normal thing in the world. That was just like Louise, Daniel thought. His mother may be his aunt, but in her world it would always be the small,

137

down-to-earth values which came first. To her this was a blip, and in the next hour she would think he was the same old Daniel just with a new mum. She could turn any mountain into a molehill. The thought made him smile, then he thought about the wedding. He really didn't want to marry her. He had to think about himself. He had to try and decide how all this would affect *him*. He couldn't be certain, but he knew one thing: he couldn't go back to his old way of living, going along with the safest option. If he married Louise, he would be back in the same place he started. Sooner or later he would have to break out and it was better to tell her now.

'We're going home,' he told Louise.

'I think I'd better leave too,' said Chris, quickly, looking glad to have seen a way out. He held his hand out awkwardly to Daniel.

'Friends?'

Daniel shook it without saying anything. Chris gave Sarah a nod in farewell and quietly left the house.

She waited till she heard Chris close the front door, then Sarah hugged Daniel tight. 'Nothing's changed,' she murmured in his ear.

'Nothing except me,' he told her.

Their eyes met. All of a sudden she looked tired and older. 'No, you haven't,' she said. 'It doesn't matter where you start. It's where you're going that counts.'

Daniel smiled. He'd managed to work that out for himself, he thought.

'That's right, Mum,' he said. 'That's exactly right.'

On the way home he told Louise that the wedding was off.

'There was something about the way you were acting,' she said. 'I thought you had cold feet. I was going to tell you we didn't have to.'

He didn't answer, thinking about how to explain.

'What are we supposed to do now?' Louise asked.

Her voice sounded normal but there were tears running down her face.

Daniel thought about saying something comforting, then decided not to.

'We're having a baby,' Daniel said, 'but you don't really know lots of things about me. How I feel. I don't want to pretend.'

Something else struck him. 'I've been so busy being the person I thought I was supposed to be that I'm not sure I know you either.'

'So what do we do?'

When Louise said that an image of Judy stretched out on the bed in front of him came into Daniel's mind. He couldn't give her up, he thought. It wasn't just Judy, though. Being with her had made him feel in control of his life. It was something about being free to do what he wanted. At the same time he knew that he couldn't let his child grow up without a father.

'Let's go on the way we are and see what happens,' he told her.

There would be plenty of time, he thought, to work out what to do. Louise was going to be hurt, he guessed, no matter what he did. But maybe she would learn to make the sort of bargain with life that he had always been forced to accept. Between them, perhaps they could change the meaning of the word 'normal'. That would be his best offer. He still didn't know what he wanted, but now he knew that he didn't have to settle for any less.

'I don't know,' Louise said. 'What shall we tell people?'

'Tell them we changed our minds, tell them anything we want. It's our life.' He paused, thinking about it. 'I don't even know who my father is and I probably never will. The woman I thought was my mother isn't but I'm still here. I'm still who I am. I don't need to be like everyone else to be me.'

'And the baby,' she said. 'Have you thought about that?'

'I have been thinking about it,' he told her. 'Let's just take it one step at a time. I'm not going anywhere but I have to be the person I want to be.'

He thought about it. Maybe Sarah had been right not to tell him until now. But everything had changed. He thought about Nancy's face in the photo. She had kept him, and if she hadn't died they would have been together. She hadn't let anything stop her living the life she wanted, though. The funny thing was that he didn't feel very sad. He felt relieved as much as anything else. His real mother, he thought, would have wanted him to live his own life, the way she had tried to.

'Don't worry about the baby,' he said. 'At least he'll know who his father is.'

1009 1010 1011 1012 1013 1014 1015
1924 1025